At the Zoo

by Catherine Peters

illustrated by Sally Noll

GReaT SouRCe
EDUCATION GROUP
A Houghton Mifflin Company

I like the monkey and the monkey likes me.

I like the bear and the bear likes me.

I like the giraffe and the giraffe likes me.

I like the tiger and the tiger likes me.

I like the alligator and the alligator likes me.

I like the elephant.

And the elephant loves me!